PRINCE DRAKEY
The Royal Art

Story by
Drake Dantzler and
Jacquetta Dantzler

Illustrated by
GAGE STUDIO

Once Upon a Time, there was a prince named Drakey. Drakey was a great prince. He was kind, smart, funny and an amazing artist.

Drakey went to town every day and painted pictures for the people in the village.
Everyone gathered around to see his beautiful paintings.
Men, women, boys, and girls, shouted from the crowds;
"Please draw a picture of me Prince Drakey", "Pick me!",
"Me next!"

Prince Drakey looked around the crowd and picked a young boy with a blue hat on. "I will draw you next". The young boy jumped with excitement.

Drakey was not just an amazing artist, he had a
special talent. He could paint blindfolded!
After he picked the boy from the crowd, he
tied his favorite blue blindfold around his eyes.
He peeked at the boy one more time, then
painted a picture that looked just like him.

The boy ran off to show his parents. They were amazed at Prince Drakey's talent.

Drakey picked a young girl with a yellow bow in her hair next. She danced with joy.

Once again, Drakey covered his eyes with his favorite blue blindfold. Peeked at the girl one more time. Then painted his masterpiece.

"WOW!" Thank you Prince Drakey I love it!" The girl rushed over to show all of her friends her painting.

"That's all for today!" Prince Drakey said as he packed up his paint supplies. "Please, just one more" a lady with a purple handkerchief cried. "What about me?!" a man with a big mustache called out.

"No worries, I will be back tomorrow. Good day!" Prince Drakey smiled and walked back to his palace. The crowd cheered and applauded as he walked away.

As promised, the next day Drakey walked to the village with his paint supplies in hand.

"Look! There he is! Prince Drakey is coming!"

The people ran over to get a front row view of Prince Drakey's artwork. They all hoped to be chosen to have their very own picture painted by the prince.

"How about you?" Drakey picked a quiet little baby who was sitting in her mother's arms. The baby had big beautiful eyes and a pink ribbon on her shirt.

Drakey took out his blue blindfold and tied it around his eyes. He lifted the blindfold to take one more look, then painted the most vivid picture of the happy baby girl.

Her parents were so thrilled. "Thank you Prince!"

He noticed a boy sitting alone. "Would you like a painting?" He asked the boy. "Yes! I would love one!"

Drakey tied his blindfold. Peeked to get one last look. Then painted the boy who was wearing an orange jacket.

"Thank you so much Prince! This is the best gift ever!"

Prince Drakey smiled and began to put his supplies away. But he noticed a beautiful girl with a very pretty teal dress. "How about one more picture?"

He put on his blindfold. But this time he didn't take one last peek. He didn't need to.

Drakey began painting. But he didn't just paint the girl, he painted a castle, a pony and a prince that looked a lot like Prince Drakey.

He gave her the painting
and she was so happy!

"Thank you Prince
Drakey! I love it!"

As he packed away his paint supplies the people cheered and applauded.

"See you tomorrow" he said. And he did. He went
back the next day and every day after.

He continued to make astonishing paintings and the crowd continued to cheer.

The girl in the teal dress came back every day too.

Made in the USA
Las Vegas, NV
01 December 2020